O9-AIC-920

THE LEGEND OF
SLEEPY HOLLOW

THE LEGEND OF

SLEEPY HOLLOW

Retold from
Washington Irving
by Jane Mason

SCHOLASTIC INC.

Based on "The Legend of Sleepy Hollow" by Washington Irving.

"The Legend of Sleepy Hollow" was first
published in 1819-1820.

This book is a work of fiction. Names, characters, places, and
incidents are either the product of the author's imagination or are
used fictitiously, and any resemblance to actual persons, living
or dead, business establishments, events, or locales is entirely
coincidental.

No part of this publication may be reproduced, stored
in a retrieval system, or transmitted in any form or by any means,
electronic, mechanical, photocopying, recording,
or otherwise, without written permission of the publisher.
For information regarding permission, write to
Scholastic Inc., Attention: Permissions Department,
557 Broadway, New York, NY 10012.

ISBN 978-0-439-22510-6

Copyright © 2001 by Jane Mason. All rights reserved.
Published by Scholastic Inc., *Publishers since 1920.*
SCHOLASTIC and associated logos are trademarks
and/or registered trademarks of Scholastic Inc.

The publisher does not have any control over and
does not assume any responsibility for author or
third-party websites or their content.

22 21 20 19 18   18 19 20 21 22 23

Printed in the U.S.A.   40

This edition first printing, September 2018

Book Design by Jennifer Rinaldi

Contents

Chapter 1

Sleepy Hollow

TARRY Town sat on the shores of the mighty Hudson River in New York State. It was a pretty town with hills and valleys, rushing streams and lush forests.

Tarry Town was a truly beautiful place. But it was also cursed. Cursed with the presence of ghouls and goblins, witches and ghosts. Many of these ghosts were not friendly. And all of them loved to terrorize the good people of Tarry Town.

Yes, there was definitely something strange in the air around Tarry Town. Folks who lived near there, and even those passing through, wandered around like they were in a dream. They saw things and heard things. They spent a lot of time thinking and talking about ghosts.

You may wonder why the place where you live is not inhabited by ghosts. I can tell you. It is because most towns are quite modern. People come and go. Things change. In those towns and villages, ghosts come out of their graves and find that their friends have moved away. There is no one left to visit — or haunt. So they stay quietly in their graves and behave themselves.

This was not the case in Tarry Town. The farmers who had settled there stayed a long time, as did their families. And so there were hauntings aplenty. . . .

Some people said the town was bewitched by a German doctor during the early days of Tarry Town's settlement. Others claimed that an old Indian chief had held his powwows there before white people arrived.

During the Revolutionary War, soldiers

from the British and American armies marched and fought in the area, and some died. It was the spirits of these men who lingered near Tarry Town. And not far from Tarry Town was a particularly haunted place called Sleepy Hollow.

At first glance, Sleepy Hollow seemed to be nothing more than a quiet, wooded valley. Giant walnut trees grew straight and tall. Lush grasses and shrubs covered the ground. And in the spring and summer, beautiful wildflowers bloomed on the banks of a bubbling stream.

But beneath its lovely exterior lay something dark and mysterious. To the untrained ear, the sound of that murmuring stream was the only noise in Sleepy Hollow. But if you knew better, or if you just listened very, very carefully, you might hear footsteps or horses' hooves — or even horrible shrieks.

Because in Sleepy Hollow, a restless ghost was almost always on the prowl.

Chapter 2

The Headless Horseman

OF all the ghosts who lingered around Sleepy Hollow, the most famous and terrifying was the Headless Horseman. Nobody knew exactly who he was. But most believed him to be the ghost of an unfortunate soldier whose head had been shot off by a cannonball during a battle in the Revolutionary War.

Unable to rest in peace, the Horseman rose from his grave in a nearby churchyard every night. He and his horse raced across the countryside to the place of his final battle.

Searching desperately for his head, the Horseman combed the battle area until it was almost daylight. Then, knowing that he must return to his grave before the sun rose, he roared back through the forests of Sleepy Hollow with his cloak flapping behind him like the wings of a giant blackbird.

Some said that the Horseman carried a pumpkin head wherever he went. It sat in front of him, resting on the saddle. Villagers claimed that the Horseman hurled this pumpkin head at anyone who got in his way.

Many people in Sleepy Hollow claimed to have had run-ins with the Headless Horseman. Some had been awoken from sleep at night by thundering hooves outside their windows. Others had been dragged on wild rides through the countryside on the back of the Horseman's black horse. Still others had been attacked as they walked home from a long day's work.

The people of Tarry Town spoke often about the Headless Horseman of Sleepy

Hollow. At parties and gatherings, children and grown-ups sat around the fireplace to hear tales of his nightly rides. When caught out after dark, the towns-people made as much noise as they could, tramping loudly through the woods.

Everyone knew it could be deadly to surprise the Headless Horseman.

Chapter 3

Ichabod Crane

IT was true that the native people of Tarry Town were obsessed with ghosts and apparitions. And most of all, they feared the Headless Horseman. But people who moved to Tarry Town from other places were also soon entranced by the spookiness of the area. After living there for only a short time, they seemed to catch the ghost fever of the land. Such was the case for young Ichabod Crane, who moved to Tarry Town from the neighboring state of Connecticut.

Ichabod was an odd man, with a smattering of talents. His life was a patchwork of many different things.

Ichabod was funny-looking. He had a

small head, big ears, and glassy green eyes. His feet were enormous. His arms and legs were unbelievably long. In fact, his hands seemed to dangle a mile below his shirtsleeves! When seen at a distance, you might have thought he was a scarecrow who had wandered out of his cornfield.

As for his work, Ichabod was first and foremost a schoolteacher. He had moved to Tarry Town to teach in the one-room schoolhouse that was located in the spooky valley of Sleepy Hollow itself.

Even though Ichabod looked funny, his students liked him. He was strict, of course. He made sure his students worked hard at their subjects: reading, writing, and arithmetic. And he was quick to punish a student who was late or was misbehaving in class. But he was also fair, and he treated everyone equally.

During recess, Ichabod sometimes played games with the older children.

And he was always willing to referee the students' games.

When the school day was over, Ichabod often spent the afternoons with his students. He helped them with their homework or fished with them in a nearby stream. And he often walked with the younger children, seeing them safely home.

Ichabod was also a singing teacher. He was proud of his voice and sang loudly — in church, when walking through the countryside, and while bathing. Ichabod loved psalms and other songs sung in church. He knew nearly all of the church songs by heart and enjoyed his job of teaching them to his students.

On Sundays, Ichabod strutted across the front of the church and took his position near the altar. His children's choir was on one side of him, the congregation on the other. While the organist played, he and his singing pupils belted out one psalm after another, with the congregation joining in. Some believed this time in church, singing, was the highlight of Ichabod's week.

Unfortunately for Ichabod, teachers were not well paid at that time. It was respectable to be a schoolmaster, but the money was not good. This could have been terrible for Ichabod, because he loved to eat. He ate so much, in fact, that everyone wondered how he stayed so skinny. He ate enough for three men. And since his paycheck was so small, he would have had to spend every last penny on food! There would be nothing left to pay for a place to live.

Luckily, the people of Tarry Town liked Ichabod, and they developed a clever system to help their hungry, poorly paid schoolmaster.

To make ends meet, Ichabod was invited to live at his pupils' homes. He would stay with one family for a week or so, then go to another, moving around until he was back with the first family once again.

Now, this setup could have caused problems. Some of the farmers didn't think school was necessary for their children. Also, they had to *pay* for their children to go to school (though it was not a lot). To house and feed the schoolmaster on top of those bothersome things was almost too much for some.

So it was a good thing that Ichabod always managed to be helpful around the farms. He helped to make hay, mend fences, water the horses, drive the cows from pasture, and cut wood for the winter fire. All of this extra help made the farmers happy, and even the grumpiest of them had to agree that Ichabod was a good man and a hard worker. So they did not mind too much when the schoolmaster devoured the food at their breakfast and dinner tables.

As for the farmers' wives, Ichabod had no trouble winning them over. He was always complimenting them on their wonderful food (after all, Ichabod would eat anything!) and was very sweet with the little children. In school he was strict and stern. But in the farmhouses he was gentle and loving. Ichabod spent many an evening with a child on his knee or rocking a cradle for hours on end.

So between teaching school subjects, singing psalms, and lodging at one local farmhouse or another, Ichabod Crane managed to live a happy, healthy life. . . .

For a time.

Chapter 4

Ghosts and Goblins

ICHABOD, along with most of the people who lived near Sleepy Hollow, was a firm believer in witches and ghosts. He had his very own copy of a book by Cotton Mather called *History of New England Witchcraft* and had read it over and over. He carried it wherever he went.

So it is not surprising that when Ichabod was not busy teaching in his schoolhouse, helping mend fences, rocking children to sleep, or wolfing down the food at farmhouse tables, he could be seen or heard sitting around farmhouse fireplaces listening to or spinning tales of ghosts and goblins. Or haunted brooks and bridges. Or bewitched barns and houses. Or anything else that went bump in the night.

Ichabod loved listening during these spooky story sessions. He loved the crackle of the fire as the storytellers' voices echoed in the near darkness. He loved the feeling of tingles running up his spine. And he loved to hear all about the Headless Horseman, a specter he himself had never actually seen.

But more than anything, Ichabod loved to tell his own stories. While the fires crackled and spat, he would tell his intent listeners about all kinds of witchcraft and omens and spells. Then he would rant about the blackness and unknown of outer space — comets and shooting stars! And, as a last shocking tale, he would burst out that the world was constantly spinning around — half the time the very town they lived in was upside down!

Of course, many of the villagers did not believe a word of Ichabod's tales about outer space or the world spinning. But they were certain that his tales of ghosts and witches were the absolute truth.

After a particularly scary tale, the conversation would bubble like a witch's brew. Eyes around the fire would shine bright. Everyone knew they were safe for a time, for no goblin or ghost would dare show itself in a cozy chimney corner full of cheerful human faces.

Then, when it was quite late — and very dark outside — everyone would head home for the night. Some villagers whistled as they climbed into their wagons. Others chatted as they strode in small groups down the path toward home.

But Ichabod did neither. He often had to walk all by himself to whatever farm housed him, and he tiptoed carefully through the woods alone. His imagination ran wild. Fear gripped his heart. Every tree, shrub, and fence post was a ghost in the dark night. His own footsteps echoed ominously in the country stillness. And each gust of wind made his blood run cold. He was certain that each time he heard a thump or a gust or a snap, it was none other than the Headless Horseman!

Of course the trees, shrubs, fence posts, and wind did not hurt Ichabod. Nor did his own footsteps. But his fear made him crazy. It was only when he finally reached the cozy farmhouse where he was staying that he felt better.

Then, as he lay in bed in the dark, Ichabod could not help listening for bumps and howls in the night. And more than once, just outside his window, Ichabod was certain he heard the galloping hooves of the Headless Horseman.

Chapter 5
Lazy Afternoons

DESPITE his terrifying walks home and the fitful nights, Ichabod went to every storytelling gathering he could. He could not help himself. He was as hungry for haunted tales as he was for food. He simply could not get enough.

When he was in class with his students, his mind was firmly focused on teaching and keeping his students in line. He made sure his students worked hard and learned their subjects well.

Once school let out, though, Ichabod's mind once again drifted to hauntings. He often spent the afternoon lying on a bed of clover, poring over Cotton Mather's *History of New England Witchcraft*.

During the day, these tales did not frighten him very much. He could read the most gruesome tale — like the one about the farmer who had been shot in the stomach and now strode through his barn with blood and intestines oozing out of his middle — and not even flinch.

But as he became more and more absorbed in the book he was reading, the afternoon always wore on. And, as it did every day, the sun would set, and a quiet hush would settle over the forest.

By the time Ichabod had closed his book and taken a good look around, the shadows were long. Dusk — that terrible in-between time when it was neither light nor dark — was upon him.

Looking around warily, Ichabod would get up from his comfortable spot and pack up his bag. *How did it get to be so late?* he would wonder as he started down the trail to the farm where he happened to be lodged.

As Ichabod made his way through Sleepy Hollow, the evening shadows always startled him. The snap of sticks under his feet raised the hair on the back of his neck. The occasional sound of a woodland creature — a moaning whippoorwill, a crying tree toad, or a screaming screech owl — sent poor Ichabod off the hard-to-see trail more than once. He often called out "who's there?" in distress.

And when Ichabod had to walk under a thick canopy of trees or past the darkest swamp or bog, a firefly almost always streamed across his path. That was a sure sign of a witch's spell.

During these terrifying trips to his temporary home, Ichabod had only one defense. Unlike on his silent walks home after a good ghost story gathering, Ichabod sang psalm tunes to drive away the evil spirits and spells. As he crept around each bush and tree, he belted out a solemn line from a favorite church song.

As he moved from one song to another, his spirits lifted. Soon, he almost forgot about the ghosts and witches of the world. His singing invariably got louder and more boisterous. His nasal voice carried over the farmlands. And in this way the good people of Tarry Town always knew that Ichabod Crane was passing by on his way home for the evening.

There was one night, however, when Ichabod stopped singing in the middle of a psalm tune. The ground under his feet was vibrating, and the sound of a galloping horse echoed in the distance.

Panicked, Ichabod started to run. But it was almost dark, and the path was hard to see. Sweat trickled down his back as the sound of the hooves came nearer and nearer. Ichabod's breath caught in his throat. A horse was almost upon him!

Ichabod rushed forward — and tripped and fell on a tree root! He was sure he was done for. But a moment later the horse and rider raced right by him in a nearby field, disappearing into the darkening night.

Still breathing heavily, Ichabod got to his feet. He was sure he had barely escaped an encounter with the Headless Horseman.

Chapter 6
Singing Lessons

WHILE some farmers in the area did not think it was important that their children go to school, everyone agreed that it was a great honor to have a child in the church choir. As a result, Ichabod had a large gathering of students each week for his singing classes.

Ichabod ran these singing lessons like he ran his regular schoolroom — strictly but fairly. If his students had little talent, he did not punish them for being off-key, but he made them practice hard just the same. And if students had a natural gift, he never let them off easily but demanded that they work equally hard at learning and performing the music.

But in spite of his overall fairness, there was one singing student whom Ichabod could not seem to criticize: eighteen-year-old Katrina Van Tassel.

Katrina was beautiful. She wore pure gold jewelry, which always looked lovely against her pale skin. Her fashionable clothes set off her plump figure. And she had a lovely singing voice.

Katrina was sweet-tempered and friendly. She was also used to getting her way. She was an only child, and her parents spoiled her. She did not practice her songs as much as she should and often did not pay attention in class. Instead, Katrina spent most of her class time flirting with the older boys.

Still, Ichabod would not criticize her. He even became flustered when he was forced to interrupt her interruptions. This was very unusual behavior for the schoolmaster. It caused his other students to wonder why he let her get away with things. They talked about it in school, at home, and in church. And soon the people of Tarry Town suspected that Ichabod Crane was smitten with Katrina Van Tassel.

Chapter 7
A Thriving Farm

ONE day Ichabod had reason to meet with Katrina's father. Before this time, Ichabod had never been to the Van Tassel farm. It was in an out-of-the-way place, and Katrina was too old to be a school student of his.

Ichabod expected the farm to be like the many others near Sleepy Hollow — comfortable and plain. So when he saw how huge and bountiful it was, his large green eyes nearly popped out of his head!

Nestled in a fertile nook of land on the shores of the Hudson River, the Van Tassel farm was anything but plain. It was an estate!

Fields of ripening crops spread in every direction: wheat, rye, buckwheat, and Indian corn. The trees in the orchards were heavy with ripened fruit: apples, pears, and pomegranates.

The barn was as big as a church, for Van Tassel had many animals. A troop of fat pigs paraded across their pen. Turkeys gobbled merrily in the courtyard. Guinea fowl shouted contentment with their strange cries. And in an adjoining pond swam ducks and a squadron of snowy geese.

Every nesting bird in the area seemed to make its home in the rafters of the huge barn. If it wasn't snuggled in its nest it was on the roof, enjoying the warm sunshine.

Not far from the barn, a clear freshwater spring bubbled up from the ground. The sweet water poured into a well made from a barrel, then spilled over and meandered through the grass to a neighboring brook.

As Ichabod looked out over the vast farm, he was overcome by an intense hunger. He imagined all of the livestock and fowl cooked into delicious stews and roasts with gravies. He could smell the orchard fruit baked into perfect pies and cakes. He wanted to sit at Mr. Van Tassel's dinner table and eat until he was too full to move.

The farmhouse itself was equally grand. The front porch held benches, tables, and a spinning wheel.

Inside the front hall, ears of Indian corn and strings of dried apples and peaches were hung along the walls. A giant bag of wool from Van Tassel's sheep sat waiting to be spun into yarn. Another bag held coarse thread ready to be woven into clothing. Polished pewter platters, vases, and other dishes covered a long dresser.

Through a slightly open door, Ichabod was able to peep into the beautiful parlor. Fancy wooden tables and claw-footed chairs were polished to a bright shine. Beautiful seashells decorated the fireplace. And a corner cupboard displayed numerous pieces of old silver and delicate china.

Ichabod was beside himself. Never had he seen such wealth. The livestock! The crops! The furniture! The china!

At that very moment, Ichabod was overtaken by greed. He wanted absolutely everything he saw to be his, including the one thing it would take to win it all: the hand of the Van Tassels' lovely daughter, Katrina.

Chapter 8
The Rival

BEFORE long, Ichabod had a plan to court and woo Katrina. Since he was her singing teacher, she already knew him. And like most of the girls, she found him to be quite interesting.

You see, most of the young men who lived in Sleepy Hollow were farmers' sons. They were gruff and awkward — country bumpkins. Compared to these young men, Ichabod was a gentleman. And perhaps more important, he was a learned gentleman. He had read several books thoroughly and was, of course, an expert on Cotton Mather's *History of New England Witchcraft*.

On top of being the schoolmaster,

Ichabod was also the choir director in church, which was a highly esteemed position.

Often after church on Sundays, the young women of the congregation would gather around Ichabod. They strolled together along the banks of the nearby millpond. Or, for their amusement, Ichabod read out loud the epitaphs on the tombstones — some of them about the unfortunate men whose ghosts still haunted the region.

Many of these girls were sweet and pretty. But after seeing the Van Tassel farm, Ichabod was interested only in Katrina. So he began to court her in earnest.

Now, the knights and princes of earlier times only had to battle giants and dragons and magic spells. But Ichabod had a *really* serious obstacle to overcome. Katrina was also being courted by the most popular Dutchman in Tarry Town: Brom Van Brunt.

Unlike Ichabod, Brom was handsome. He had broad shoulders and curly black hair. His sturdy frame and brute strength had earned him the name Brom Bones, which was what everyone called him.

Brom Bones was an expert horseback rider. He was always the one to settle a dispute among the men, and no one ever disputed him. Brom was constantly playing practical jokes and stirring up trouble, but it was always in fun.

If anything, Brom's crazy behavior made him even more popular. After all, he always had a colorful story to tell. But some people wondered if he only *appeared* to be so popular because no one dared to go against him.

Brom traveled with four or five equally tough and manly companions. They looked up to him and did whatever he wanted. The noisy bunch could often be heard whooping and hollering as they rode home late after an evening of pranks at the local tavern. Villagers would remark when they heard him pass, "There goes Brom Bones."

While some said that the attention that Brom paid to Katrina was quite gruff (he was not, after all, a gentleman), rumor had it that she did not discourage him. And his horse, Daredevil, was often seen tied to a Van Tassel fence post in the evenings.

Because of Brom, most of the men of Tarry Town gave up all hope of winning Katrina. Surely Brom Bones would lead her to the altar. Ichabod, though, did not give up. He was not stupid enough to approach Katrina in front of Brom, of course. But under the guise of being her singing teacher, he often visited her at her farmhouse.

Luckily for Ichabod, Katrina's parents

did not stand in his way. Her father doted on his only child. He always let her have her way. If she were to choose Ichabod, or anyone else for that matter, that would be fine with him.

Katrina's mother, for her part, was very busy running the house and managing her huge collection of fowl and poultry. Besides, she reasoned, girls could take care of themselves. It was the chickens that needed looking after.

So while Katrina's father sat on the front porch smoking his pipe and her mother bustled about the house, Ichabod had Katrina all to himself. Together they took long walks across the fields or sat by the side of the spring under the giant elm tree.

Soon after Ichabod began making his advances, Brom Bones stopped coming to the Van Tassels'. Ichabod was delighted by this.

But before long, a kind of feud erupted

between Ichabod and the popular Dutchman. Brom would have fought Ichabod openly and with his fists. Ichabod, of course, knew quite well that Brom would win such a fight. So he decided to fight the battle in other ways. Namely, he avoided Brom at all costs. And he wisely went near Katrina only when he knew Brom was nowhere nearby.

This system worked quite well for Ichabod. But there was a catch: Ichabod became the brunt of Brom's practical jokes and mischievous doings. There was the time Brom and his men broke into the schoolhouse and turned everything topsy-turvy. The place was such a mess that Ichabod thought witches were holding their meetings in his own schoolhouse!

Worse, Brom made Ichabod look like a fool in front of Katrina. He trained a stray dog to whine and howl whenever

Ichabod tried to teach Katrina a new psalm. The dog was so loud that neither Katrina nor Ichabod could hear anything else.

And then there was the night that Brom and his gang followed Ichabod home after he'd been visiting Katrina. Ichabod was strolling happily through the woods, barely noticing that night was upon him, when the sound of galloping hooves suddenly surrounded him.

Terrified, Ichabod began to run, but soon stopped in his tracks. A towering black steed was standing in his path. A moment later, a large orange pumpkin sailed through the air, smashing into the ground just a few inches from Ichabod's feet.

Ichabod stood rooted to the path, frozen with fear. It was not until he heard Brom's rumbling laughter that he had the courage to continue on his way home.

Even so, he looked over his shoulder more than once before he got to the farmhouse where he was staying.

Some of Brom's pranks were terrifying. If Ichabod hadn't been dead set on marrying Katrina, he might have given up out of fear. But he was determined. And he seemed to be winning the lady over. If things kept going his way, he'd soon have Katrina's heart and hand — and the vast Van Tassel farm.

Chapter 9

An Invitation

ONE warm autumn afternoon, Ichabod sat in his schoolroom while his students worked away at their seats. The room was quiet, and soft afternoon light filtered through the window. Ichabod's desk was full of items he had recently taken from his more devious students: a half-munched apple, two whirligigs, a fly cage, and several paper animals.

Ichabod was thinking about the fate of his relationship with Katrina when a clattering of hooves caught his attention. A burly man on a wild-looking colt raced up to the schoolhouse, jumped down, and tied his horse to a railing. A moment later the messenger came thundering into the schoolhouse.

While the students looked up in surprise (interruptions at the schoolhouse were very rare), Ichabod hurried to the door to see what the man was after. The man grinned and handed Ichabod an invitation. It was not just any invitation, either, but one to a quilting frolic at the farm of none other than Mr. Van Tassel.

Ichabod was filled with glee, and the rest of the afternoon the schoolhouse was full of bustle and hubbub. The students were hurried through their lessons. Books were flung aside without being put neatly back on the shelves. Inkstands were turned over. Benches were knocked down and not picked up. And the entire class was let out an hour early. The students tore out of the schoolhouse in excitement. Their whoops and hollers echoed across the hollow as they ran and jumped in the autumn sun.

With the schoolhouse finally empty, Ichabod took his time getting ready for the party. Using a small piece of broken glass that hung in the back of the room as a mirror, he spent a very long time primping and preening. He brushed and shined his best (and only) black suit. He combed his hair this way and that. And he straightened his tie at least six times.

When he was finally satisfied with his reflection, he set off to the farm where he was staying. He had a strong feeling that tonight would be an important night with Katrina, and he wanted to borrow a horse to make a good impression on her.

Hans Van Ripper, the owner of the farm where Ichabod was staying, was happy to oblige the schoolmaster. So Ichabod set forth, riding a horse to the Van Tassel farm.

To be honest, it must be told that the animal Ichabod rode was actually an ancient, broken-down plow horse. He was gaunt and shaggy, with a skinny neck and a thick head. His mane and tail were tangled and matted with burrs. One eye was missing a pupil, and the other had a remarkably evil gleam!

Gunpowder, as the horse was called, had once been a favorite of his master's. And as Van Ripper was a fast and furious rider, it was thought that he had given his horse some of his own spirit. For as old as Gunpowder was, he still had a devilish spark about him.

Ichabod was a good match for the funny-looking steed, for he, too, looked odd. He rode with very short stirrups, which brought his knees clear up to his chest. His bony elbows stuck out like a grasshopper's legs. As Gunpowder jogged along, Ichabod's arms flapped like a pair of wings. And the skirts of his black coat fluttered back, practically to the horse's matted tail.

Ichabod thought himself quite gallant

as he rode along the trail to Katrina's house. But together with Gunpowder he was quite a strange sight — not very unlike some of the ghosts who wandered Sleepy Hollow in the dead of night!

Chapter 10

Feasting and Merriment

AFTER a lovely ride through the colorful countryside, Ichabod arrived at the Van Tassel estate. It was mobbed by the people of Tarry Town, who had come to celebrate autumn.

The farmers were dressed in their homespun coats and pants and wore polished pewter buckles. The farmers' wives wore ruffled hats and long-waisted dresses with scissors and pincushions hanging on the outside. The young women were dressed like their mothers, but sported straw hats or fine ribbons in their hair. And the young men wore short coats with rows of shiny brass buttons.

Brom Bones was the hero of the party. He arrived on his horse, Daredevil — a horse so wild and mischievous that he alone caused a stir. And, of course, Brom was dressed in his best. As Ichabod made his way to the farmhouse, he spied a group of girls already gathering around Brom.

Once inside, though, Ichabod forgot all about Brom Bones. His eye was caught not by Katrina or any other damsel but by the amazing bounty of the buffet table. His eyes bugged out at the very sight of it, and his mouth began to water.

The table was covered with platters of every food imaginable. There were all kinds of Dutch tea cakes: the doughy doughnut, the tender *oly koek,* the crisp and crumbling cruller, sweet cakes and shortcakes, ginger cakes and honey cakes.

Mixed in with the cake platters were all kinds of pies, sliced ham and roast beef, delectable dishes of preserved peaches and pears, broiled shad and roast chickens, and bowls of milk and cream!

Standing tall among it all was a giant teapot that sent up clouds of vapor from its magnificent spout.

Ichabod had worked up quite an appetite during his ride to the farm, and now he hastily made his way to the table and began to eat. He ate and ate and ate, sampling everything that the incredible buffet had to offer.

Good food always made Ichabod happy. As he looked around, he could not help but think that someday all of this would be his. Ichabod licked his fingers at the end of his delicious meal and felt wonderful indeed.

Just then the sound of music echoed through the front hall, and Ichabod gleefully made his way to the common room. It was time to dance!

What many people didn't know about

Ichabod Crane was that he prided himself on his dancing as much as on his singing. He was a wonderful dancer. When the music played, all of his physical awkwardness disappeared. Every part of his body moved to the music.

Katrina was Ichabod's dance partner. As he glided gracefully across the floor, she smiled graciously at his compliments and dance moves. Indeed, the schoolmaster was the envy of every young lad in the room — especially Brom, who sat sulking by himself in a corner.

As Ichabod gazed at Katrina on the dance floor that night, he was sure he had died and gone to heaven. But that was yet to come. . . .

Chapter 11

More Ghostly Tales

WHEN the dancing was over, Ichabod joined a group of farmers and their wives out on the porch. They were telling stories about the Revolutionary War and gossiping about local hauntings.

One of the farmers, Doffue Martling, was a large, bearded Dutchman. He rambled on and on about his heroics during a terrible battle. He'd almost overtaken an enemy warship all by himself. From behind the flimsy protection of a temporary mud fortress, he'd fired his iron nine-pounder. But on the final firing the gun had broken, and he'd had to run for his life.

There was also the tale of the Battle of

White Plains. A master of defense in battle, this hero had fended off a musket ball with nothing but a small sword. The man declared that he had felt the musket ball whiz by his head — right before it had hit the base of the sword!

Each man who told a story about the war was sure that he himself had had a hand in helping America win its freedom. They shouted and pounded fists and declared that they were the best soldiers in the land.

But even the drama of the war stories was nothing compared to the tales of ghosts and apparitions that followed.

One ghost story told of the great tree where Major Andre had been killed in battle. Every night since his death a ghostly funeral train passed by the great old tree. The ghosts were hideous and miserable, and their howls and wailings could be heard for miles.

Then there was the story of the woman

in white. She had perished near Raven Rock during a bitter winter storm. Now her gruesome spirit meandered through the little valley on cold winter nights. And before a storm, you could hear her shrieks carried along by the fiercely whipping wind.

But of all the ghost tales told at Mr. Van Tassel's party, none were as terrifying as those about the Headless Horseman.

Rumor had it that the Headless Horseman had been out and about more than usual lately. He continued to patrol the country, looking for his head and tying his horse to a tree in the Sleepy Hollow graveyard every night.

Near the graveyard was a wooden bridge that crossed a babbling brook. A thick mass of trees covered both the bridge and the road that led to it. During the day the bridge was a spooky place. At night it was downright terrifying. It was also the favorite haunt of the Headless Horseman.

The first Headless Horseman tale was the one about Old Brouwer, who had always insisted there were no such things as ghosts. Apparently the Headless Horseman wanted to prove Brouwer wrong. One evening Brouwer was returning from Sleepy Hollow and met the Horseman. The ghost commanded that Brouwer get up on his horse with him. Terrified for his life, Brouwer obliged.

Together the two roared across the countryside on the back of the black steed. The horse traveled so fast that Brouwer could barely tell where they were. When they reached the bridge near the graveyard, the Headless Horseman suddenly turned into a glowing skeleton. With a bony hand he pushed Old Brouwer into the brook, then disappeared over the treetops with a booming clap of thunder.

While most of the listening crowd nodded gravely at the end of the tale, there was one man who burst out laughing. It was Brom Bones, who had his own tale of the Headless Horseman.

Being an expert rider himself, Brom was quick to refer to the Headless Horseman as some sort of inexperienced rider. Brom told about the time he had come across the Headless Horseman upon his return from a neighboring village. The Horseman wanted to race with him — for a bowl of punch. Of course, Brom was willing to take the bet.

The two tore through the night at lightning speed, over fences and fallen trees, through forests and across fields. Brom was riding Daredevil and declared that the Horseman's steed was no match for his horse's incredible speed. Brom was about to win the race as they came to the church bridge. But a second later, just before the bridge, the Headless Horseman disappeared in a flash of fire.

The people oohed and whispered to one another when Brom finished his story.

"A flash of fire," someone whispered.

"Into thin air," said another.

"Gone, but due to return," muttered a third.

Ichabod, having heard Brom's tale, felt pressed to add his own stories to the mix. He rambled on about the mischievous events that he had witnessed in his home state of Connecticut as well as the fearful sights he had seen in his walks through Sleepy Hollow.

As he wove his tales of dread, poor Ichabod did not know that the most fearsome sight of all was still to come.

Chapter 12

Into the Night

LATE in the night, the Van Tassel party broke up. The farmers gathered their families in their wagons and set out over the hills and fields. Some of the young men sat their ladies on their horses and they cheerfully rode off together.

Ichabod remained behind to visit with Katrina, as was the custom. While he waited for her, he whistled happily. He was sure that he was on the road to success.

When Ichabod came out of the meeting with Katrina, though, it was clear that something had gone wrong. Nobody knows exactly what happened, because the meeting had been private. But when Ichabod appeared again, he did not smile. He did not pause to grab a last morsel from the overflowing tea table. He did not gaze lovingly at the beautiful farmhouse.

Ichabod went straight to the stable and roughly woke old Gunpowder, who was enjoying a restful snooze in a cozy stall. Climbing upon the back of the shaggy horse, Ichabod kicked Gunpowder's flanks — hard — and rode off into the black night.

Ichabod seemed to be so upset over Katrina that he didn't notice how dark it was. As he rode along the banks of the Hudson, blackness surrounded him. A dog barked in the faraway distance, but there were no signs of life nearby. Ichabod slumped in his saddle. He was all alone.

The night grew darker and darker. The stars seemed to sink deeper into the sky.

As Ichabod approached a familiar place in the road, his mind flooded with the stories he had heard just a few hours earlier.

Towering over him was Major Andre's tree. Its limbs were bigger than most tree trunks, and they were viciously gnarled. They twisted down practically to the ground before twisting right back into the air.

Suddenly afraid, Ichabod began to whistle. For a moment he thought his whistle had been answered. But it was only the wind whipping through the massive tree.

Looking up, Ichabod saw a white figure above him. He inhaled sharply. But it was only a place in the trunk where lightning had struck and revealed the white wood.

Groans echoed around Ichabod, and his teeth began to chatter. Was it a member of the infamous funeral train?

No, it had only been two of the tree branches rubbing together.

Ichabod heaved a sigh of relief as he rode on, leaving the tree behind him. He was safe.

But he still had a long ride ahead.

Chapter 13
The Last Ride

NOT far from Andre's tree, a small brook crossed the road. The brook trickled into a marshy area known as Wiley's Swamp. Rough-cut logs formed a kind of bridge over the brook. And like the bridge near the Sleepy Hollow cemetery, the area around the bridge was overgrown with bushes and vines. It was a very gloomy place.

Crossing the bridge at night was a challenge for even the bravest soul. For this was the exact spot where Major Andre had been taken. The men who had done him in had hidden in the thick undergrowth.

Ichabod steeled his resolve and gave

Gunpowder a firm kick to urge him quickly onward. But instead of sprinting across the bridge, the wayward horse started to the side and crashed sideways into a fence.

Furious and afraid, Ichabod tightened the reins and kicked the horse even harder. But the horse started off in the opposite direction — straight into a thicket of thorny bushes.

Tightening the reins further still, Ichabod kicked Gunpowder a third time. The horse dashed forward, snuffing and snorting. But a second later he stopped short, right in front of the bridge. Ichabod nearly flew over the horse's head.

At that moment something stomped in the water on the other side of the bridge. In the dark shadows next to the water Ichabod spotted a figure: huge, towering, black, and misshapen.

The figure did not move. It simply stood there, as if waiting for its prey.

The hair on the back of Ichabod's neck rose again. What could he do? If he tried to flee, the figure would certainly catch him.

Summoning all of his courage, Ichabod cleared his throat and said, "Who are you?"

The apparition did not answer. So Ichabod asked again. Still the figure was silent.

Ichabod kicked Gunpowder, and the horse started across the bridge. As a panicked Ichabod neared the black figure, he did the only thing he could think of. He broke into a psalm tune.

The black figure moved. Suddenly it was in the middle of the road, straight ahead.

Though the night was very dark, Ichabod could now see that the figure was a horseman of some kind. Both the horse and the rider were large and strong-looking.

Ichabod kept a tight rein on Gunpowder and urged the horse forward, around the figure. But the silent black horseman followed him. Ichabod slowed his horse, but the other rider did the same.

Ichabod had momentarily stopped singing and now wanted to start again. But his mouth was so dry he could not squeak out a single note. As the dark rider continued to follow him, Ichabod's heart sank in his chest. He was in terrible trouble.

And then, as they came over a little hill and into open air, Ichabod turned and got a better look at the horseman. Unable to stop himself, he gasped loudly.

The man was headless, and a pumpkin head was riding on the saddle in front of its owner. Ichabod Crane was face-to-face with the Headless Horseman of Sleepy Hollow!

Ichabod shuddered in horror and

kicked Gunpowder — hard. His horse took off at a gallop, but the other steed was quick to follow. The two raced through the inky night, sending up dirt and stones.

Ichabod's clothes fluttered behind him as he leaned forward on his horse, pressing the animal on. But the Headless Horseman was fast and had no trouble keeping up.

Finally, Ichabod came to the fork in the road that led to Sleepy Hollow. Just at the fork, Gunpowder made an abrupt turn and plunged downhill — heading straight for the Headless Horseman's bridge!

Ichabod tried to remain calm. But during his frantic ride, Gunpowder's saddle had somehow gotten loose. Now it was falling off!

Ichabod made a desperate attempt to hold the saddle on the horse. It was no use. He had a single second to grab

Gunpowder around the neck before the saddle crashed to the ground. A moment later, he heard the Headless Horseman trample over it.

For a split second Ichabod worried about the wrath of Hans Van Ripper. It was his good saddle. But a snort from the black steed on his heels reminded him that he had a much bigger problem to worry about.

Still clutching Gunpowder's neck, Ichabod quickly looked up. The bridge was just a short way ahead, and beyond it was the church.

Ichabod remembered the story Brom Bones had told at the Van Tassel party. The Headless Horseman had vanished at the bridge. If Ichabod could just make it that far, he would be safe.

But the black steed was closing in, its hot breath blowing on Ichabod's neck.

Ichabod kicked Gunpowder yet again, and the old horse sprang across the bridge. Ichabod looked back to see the Horseman vanish in a flash of smoke and light.

But he didn't. Instead, the Headless Horseman rose up in his stirrups — and hurled his horrid pumpkin head at Ichabod!

Ichabod ducked, but it was too late. He was hit on the back of the head. A second later he crashed to the ground.

Chapter 14

The Mystery of Ichabod Crane

THE next morning, Gunpowder appeared at his master's gate. He wore no saddle. His bridle was helter-skelter.

Ichabod Crane did not appear for breakfast. He was not at the supper table. His students gathered at the schoolhouse, but there was no one to teach them.

By the end of the day, Hans Van Ripper began to worry. He was worried about Ichabod and also about his beautiful saddle. A search party was organized. Traveling on foot, they scoured the area.

It did not take them long to find the traces of the previous night's events.

Van Ripper's Sunday saddle was trampled in the mud. Ichabod's hat was lying on the edge of the brook, next to the deep black water. And next to the hat lay a shattered pumpkin.

The brook was carefully searched. But the body of Ichabod Crane was never found. His few worldly possessions — some clothes, a book of psalm tunes, a broken pitch pipe, and of course, Cotton Mather's *History of New England Witchcraft* — were thrown away. The school was moved to another part of Sleepy Hollow.

Naturally, the people of Tarry Town talked a lot about the fate of poor Ichabod. Gossips and gazers gathered in the churchyard on Sundays and at the edge of the brook where the pumpkin and Ichabod's hat were found.

The tales of Old Brouwer and Brom Bones were repeated. And when all had been told and retold, the people of

Sleepy Hollow came to the conclusion that poor Ichabod had been carried off by the Headless Horseman of Sleepy Hollow.

But there were other rumors about what had happened to Ichabod as well. One local farmer was positive that the schoolmaster was so afraid of running into the Headless Horseman again that he had simply left town. The farmer reported that Ichabod had moved to New York. He had supposedly become a lawyer and a politician and was doing very well for himself.

As for Brom Bones, he escorted Katrina Van Tassel to the altar shortly after Ichabod's disappearance. And whenever Brom heard folks talk about Ichabod and the Headless Horseman — especially the part about the pumpkin — he would laugh out loud. Some people believed that Brom knew a lot more about the disappearance of Ichabod than he would admit, but nobody could prove it.

The old Dutch housewives held firm. Whenever any discussion about Ichabod's disappearance arose, they declared that he had been carried off by the Headless Horseman.

By now, the story of Ichabod Crane has become quite famous. It's an old favorite, guaranteed to bring chills when told around a crackling fire on a cold winter's night.

As the people of Tarry Town head home after a night of terrible tales, they often hear galloping hooves echoing in the night. And those who listen very closely might sometimes even hear a low, sad psalm tune carried along by the wind, the long-forgotten voice of Ichabod Crane.